# Contents

# Queen Dalia Char

*A Novella Retelling the Tale of Rose Red*

Novella Two of *After the Tales and Princess-*
*A Set of Novellas*

## Aleese Hughes

ISBN: 9798685411303

# *Dedication*

To my sister Albany, for not only reading but also loving every single book I publish.

# Before you Read

This novella is about a character from the second book of *The Tales and Princesses Series*. For best enjoyment, *Apples and Princess* (Book Two) should be read before this novella.

# Chapter 1

Queen Dalia lay sprawled on her springy yet soft mattress. She stiffened her limbs as the old, snippy, new lady-in-waiting tried to pull her into a standing position.

"This. Is. Not. Very. Becoming. Your. Majesty." The woman spat each word through gritted teeth as she clawed at the Queen's legs.

Dalia sighed and relented to the frustrated pulling. Her feet touched the carpet gingerly, and she took in a deep breath before making eye contact with the Lady.

Lady Violetta Grisham hadn't always been a noblewoman. She married a lord and took over his entire estate at the time of his death barely a month after their wedding. Some rumors suggested *she* killed her husband for the riches, and Dalia wouldn't put it past her.

When the Queen finally set her jaw and dared to meet the woman's beady, black eyes, she grimaced at the sight before her. The old woman had her arms crossed tightly over her flat chest and had a deep scowl on her face, setting in the frown wrinkles at her mouth and making her skin sag past her chin.

"It is your *wedding* day, Your Majesty. Tardiness is

not an option."

Oh, how Dalia missed Lady Aeryn. Sure, she had never been afraid to talk to the Queen as if she were a normal, regular person, but Dalia and Aeryn had also been best friends. Aeryn had been encouraging, loving, and always knew what to say. Her death was still hard for Dalia to accept. Especially with a snobby, old woman standing in Aeryn's place and treating Dalia like a child.

"Let's start with the dress," Lady Violetta grumbled.

Dalia looked down at her pale pink nightgown, saddened by the thought of taking off the soft satin and dressing into her uncomfortable wedding dress. She had only tried it on once before— the day she was *supposed* to get married... The day of not only Aeryn's death but of that Snow White's, as well. That terrible day had been weeks ago, but Dalia felt as if the events were fresh in her mind.

After Lady Violetta slipped the white gown's rough lace over Dalia's unkempt, fiery curls, the Queen gazed at herself in the full-length mirror before her and winced. They still hadn't fixed the gapping in the dress's bust. However, it was a gorgeous gown with its elaborate twirlings of flowers and vines dressing the large skirt and climbing up the bodice. But regardless of its beauty, the ensemble's stark white made her bright, red hair stick out even more than it usually did, which Dalia absolutely hated. She didn't like to stick out more than she already had to as the Queen.

"You look lovely."

Dalia started from the compliment. Lady Violetta didn't seem the type to say such things. Without granting a reply to the statement, Dalia glared at her reflection for a moment, then quickly turned away at the intensity of her own brilliant, green eyes. She didn't seem to care whether she looked pretty or not. The Queen didn't feel any more excitement on this day than she had the original wedding date. She knew Prince Frederik didn't love her, and Dalia also knew she could never love him. Not after everything that had happened between him and Snow White.

"I know what you're thinking, Your Majesty."

Dalia could barely hear Lady Violetta's gravelly tone over her own thoughts.

"What was that?"

The lady-in-waiting gripped Dalia's narrow shoulders, digging her long nails into her bare skin, and turned the Queen around less than gently.

"You do not wish to be married."

Her beady, dark eyes bore into the Queen's, and Dalia felt a shiver down her spine.

"Oh?" the Queen squeaked. "Why do you say that?"

Lady Violetta clicked her tongue. "You're as pale as a sheet, and I've seen more excitement from a single kitchen maid for the day's events than I have from you."

"I'm not one to get giddy over things," Dalia said, shrugging.

The Lady raised a penciled brow, opened her

mouth to say more, but then decided against pushing the subject. Dalia felt her tense muscles begin to relax. How could she explain her feelings to anyone, let alone someone so seemingly cold?

Dalia flinched at the touch of Lady Violetta's cold hands slapping at her cheeks.

"We need to get some color back into that face of yours." She stepped back and studied the Queen with displeasure. "Nothing a little rouge can't fix, I guess. Come, Your Majesty. Let's finish getting ready."

# Chapter 2

Dalia could hear the excited chatter of hundreds of guests behind the looming doors of the throne room. She didn't have to listen to know what her subjects and visitors were whispering about: A royal wedding was always quite the ordeal. They were admiring the dozens of flower arrangements scattered across the spacious room. Many giggled at the nervous groom atop the dais and speculated how the Queen would look when she entered through the tall doors.

Dalia looked down at herself. She knew she looked more beautiful than she ever had. That had been not only Lady Violetta's intention, but also the seamstresses, and the maids that had done her hair as Lady Violetta piled on powders to Dalia's face. Yes, she knew the crowd inside would be pleased to see such a lovely bride, but Dalia didn't care. All she could think of was the man at the end of the aisle she was expected to bind herself to. She began to wring her trembling hands together and gulped audibly.

"If you shake anymore, your dress will fall off of you!" Lady Violetta hissed from behind. She yanked the long train of Dalia's gown in her hands just hard enough to make the Queen stumble.

It took every bit of strength the Queen had not to shoot an annoyed look at the old woman. Dalia didn't need to give the Lady another reason for more chastisement.

Dalia jumped at the sound of the heavy doors opening just wide enough for one of the guards inside to poke his round head out.

"They're ready for you, Your Majesty." His voice was a lot higher than his gruff demeanor might have suggested.

Dalia bit her lip to keep it from trembling and gave him a curt nod. The guard gave her a friendly, encouraging smile, then heaved the cherry-stained doors open with a slight grunt. The hairs on the Queen's bare arms stood up as a rush of cold air met her from inside. Tears bit at her eyes from nerves, causing her vision to blur before adjusting to the sight before her.

Queen Dalia had been in the throne room *many* times before. It was already elaborately decorated with its tapestries displaying the leafless tree, emblem of Edristan, and the kingdom's brilliant blue and white colors. But the new wedding decor before her instantly took her breath away. Along the aisle beneath her feet was a deep red rug that stretched its way across to the dais at the spacious room's end. The carpet was littered with shining, white petals of daisies— her favorite flower. And every inch of the walls surrounding the room was lined with overflowing bowls and vases of daisies and lavender. There was even a splash of the color blue present from a few carnations littering the arrangements. The royal decorators truly had done a marvelous job creating such splendor and beauty.

The sight was so overpowering that it took a second for Dalia to remember where she was and notice the hundreds of pairs of eyes resting on her. Every face before her was glowing as they beamed at the beautiful bride.

Dalia gulped again and moved her gaze to the groom standing at the end of the aisle. Prince Frederik stood tall, hands clasped behind his back. Everything about him looked regal, as always. The shining white color of his suit eerily matched the daisies poking out of his left breast pocket, and his black hair was stark against the pale hues of the decorated room.

Prince Frederik was a handsome man— a *very* handsome man. There was no denying that fact, and Dalia herself had recognized his superior physical appearance quickly after they met. How could she not? But now, as she locked eyes with him, Dalia couldn't feel the butterflies she once had those first few days of courtship.

Frederik held nothing but sadness in his ocean-blue gaze as the Queen slowly approached him, her steps in rhythm to the stringed instruments playing a slow ballad in the left corner. Dalia knew the Prince didn't feel romantically towards her— he was mourning the dead Snow White. That girl and her alluring (though deceitful) charms and beauty were the only things to have captured his heart in the past few months.

Dalia didn't realize she had come to a stop before Lady Violetta gave another little tug on the Queen's train.

"Your Majesty," she hissed through the corner of her mouth, "keep moving!"

The Queen couldn't move her limbs as they slowly started to go numb. She stood, frozen, in the middle of the aisle. The musicians stopped playing the wedding march, and the guests began whispering confusedly to one another.

"I can't," she whispered.

Dalia heard the surprised chatter increase. "What? What did she say?" she heard all around her.

"I can't!" Dalia cried, surprising herself, along with all those surrounding her.

Prince Frederik flinched at the shout, then ashamedly brought his gaze to his feet. He seemed sorrowful, but not because he wanted the wedding to continue— Dalia knew that he felt her hesitation was his fault.

The young priest standing beside the Prince cleared his throat loudly. "Uh, shall we proceed, Your Majesty?"

Her mind went blank, and time seemed to stand still as a roaring emptiness rang in her ears. Dalia was barely able to process the priest's question.

"No."

The entire room simultaneously gasped, but Dalia felt herself grow determined. Without a second thought, Dalia hiked up her massive skirts, whirled around on her heel, then sprinted away... Past Lady Violetta, down the long aisle, and back out the opened doors.

# Chapter 3

Dalia was surprised at her ability to unlace her cumbersome gown and pull it off all by herself, even with her trembling hands. She began pacing her chambers in nothing but her shift, ignoring her toes catching at the snags on her aging rug. Asking for its replacement had been something she had failed to do.

"I can't do it, I can't do it..." Dalia muttered to herself, rubbing her bare arms against the chill in the room. The fire in her hearth had been put out long before the wedding.

Dalia threw her neck back and whimpered out a small cry. She squinted her eyes shut and pounded them with her fists. She *hated* Prince Frederik. She couldn't help it. He had betrayed her with someone else she couldn't help but despise... that Snow White.

Dalia's lip began to tremble. Feeling such strong, negative emotions for other people was not something she was used to. But she couldn't go through with this marriage. Many times in the last few weeks, Dalia had tried to convince herself that she and the Prince could move forward and learn to love each other, but the unknown terrified the Queen.

What if she would have to live in a loveless marriage for the rest of her life?

Dalia slowly opened her eyes and gazed at the painted ceiling her mother had requested for her imaginative child. That was *long* before her mother's death and *long* before Dalia had ever known sorrow as she had felt the last few months. The elaborate depictions of stars and galaxies might have once calmed her, but at that moment, Dalia couldn't steady the turmoil happening within her.

The sound of the metal doorknob jiggling frantically startled the Queen from her reverie. She quickly glanced over at the brass key resting on her vanity. Dalia had rushed away from the wedding and to her chambers as quickly as she could, then locked the door, hoping no one would catch up to her. She needed to be alone.

"Your Majesty?"

Dalia could hear Lady Violetta's shrill voice pierce through the thick walls. The Queen held her breath and didn't reply.

"Queen Dalia, you need to let me in *right* now!"

Dalia flinched at the Lady's rise in volume but otherwise didn't budge. However, once she did move, Dalia tiptoed to her looming wardrobe in the corner next to her vanity and threw the wooden doors open. Lady Violetta continued to pound on the door as Dalia sifted through the numerous ballgowns and simple (yet still elegant) dresses hanging on the rack within the wardrobe. There were dozens, and that wasn't even including the ones that rotated in and out every week. The servants that dressed the Queen always wanted her to look fresh and new. If Dalia actually counted, she probably had about one-hundred dresses. And then, every year, a new set of clothing was tailored for her. Again, it was the desire to keep the way she dressed up-to-date and stylish.

Dalia never cared for such things, but there was one outfit she had specifically asked for one year, the one she was looking for. Tucked away in the back and coated in bits of dust was her riding outfit. It was simple, lightweight, and comfortable— all requests she had made when taking the idea to the castle seamstress. She pulled it out swiftly and shook off the dust from its soft cloth. Dalia treasured her time in the outdoors with the royal horses. Still, the dress hadn't been worn in weeks, Dalia having been too busy as the new Queen to go out riding nearly as much as she used to. And not having Aeryn, her late riding companion, contributed to her lack of time spent with the beautiful horses she loved.

Dalia glanced quickly at the pile of white satin and lace that made up her wedding dress sitting on her bed in a messy heap. Then she looked to the simplistic dress in her trembling hands. Shaking her head, she threw the clothing over her body, then studied herself in the tall mirror before her. The A-line skirt flattered her narrow hips, and the black of the dress accentuated the green in her eyes.

As she stared back at her reflection, the Queen's thoughts went back to the time that mysterious witch gifted her a magical looking glass on her Coronation day. It had been a beautiful piece, with a golden frame of vines and roses, but it was also cursed. The witch Bavmorda may have intended the mirror as a gift, but Dalia only looked back on it as a cursed object that had changed her life for the worse. She squinted her eyes shut and tried to avoid thinking about that first time she had seen the fair Snow White in the mirror. She didn't know the fair maiden would one day charm away Prince Frederik, then bring about Aeryn's untimely death, initially intending to kill the Queen herself. Dalia had destroyed the piece soon after the dark events. She threw it out of her chamber window and happily watched it fall the four stories and shatter on the cobblestones below. But even with the absence of the mirror, her dark memories still remained.

Dalia sifted through the wardrobe once again and pulled out a long, equally simple cloak that matched her dress and leather riding boots to complete the outfit. As Dalia spun the cloak around her shoulders and slipped into the boots, she jumped at the sound of more knocking. It was increasingly hurried and more frantic than before. She sighed, squared her shoulders, then stormed towards her door. Dalia flung it open, making her lady-in-waiting lose her balance and nearly fall straight onto her pointed nose.

Before Lady Violetta could regain her footing, Dalia bolted out of the doorway and down the lengthy corridor, flaming hair slowly falling out of the curls pinned to her head for the wedding. Any servant she passed merely stepped out of her way as she reached the spiraling staircase. They even let her pass as she sped through the castle entryway with its glowing chandelier and slick, marble floor. She sighed in relief as she made it outside and headed to the royal stables. Dalia was grateful she hadn't run into any advisors that might have stopped her and forced her back into the wedding.

The stables were about a mile out from the castle grounds, but she had made it in just a few minutes, having alternated from a jog to a sprint the entire way. She trudged up to the swinging doors of the large, wooden building, huffing and cheeks red from the exertion of escaping the castle.

She stared at the pretty, deep red staining of the building in front of her for a moment. She couldn't exactly remember the last time she had made a visit to the stables and the horses... Had it been with Aeryn soon before her death?

Dalia shook her head and forced away the threat of tears. She heaved the doors open, causing them to swing so far and bang against the walls inside. The dozens of horses resting in the many stalls whinnied in fright from the sudden sound. The stable boy dozing off in the far corner, maybe one-hundred feet in front of the Queen, leapt out of his small stool, the banging open of the doors startling him along with the horses. His little, black cap fell off his head from the abrupt movement, revealing his tussled, mousy brown hair. His thin, freckled face flushed a deep red as he saw who had entered.

"Y-y-your Majesty!" the young man stammered, clumsily giving the Queen a bow. Dalia dismissed the gesture with a wave of her hand.

"I need a horse," she said. "I don't care which one."

The stable boy stood frozen with his mouth still agape, clutching his cap tightly in his white hands.

"Quickly!" Dalia looked over her shoulder nervously. She was sure someone would catch up to her any minute.

The boy closed his mouth shut and jumped into action. His shaking hands fumbled with a steel lock at the stall closest to him. The horse inside began neighing with excitement, as if he knew he was about to come out for a ride.

Dalia tapped her foot impatiently, craning her neck to try to see which horse the stable boy was retrieving for her. The Queen's favorite was usually Flicker, a beautiful white mare with a substantial amount of spirit and loyalty to Dalia, but she didn't have time to request the beast. Flicker took more time than the average horse to be saddled up, usually protesting against such things by thrashing and kicking out at the person working with her. Dalia could usually calm Flicker down pretty well, but she needed to get out quickly. She wanted enough time to ride out into the woods and think through things before someone would inevitably catch up and bring her back. And then the wedding would probably be rescheduled.

Dalia felt her stomach churn at the thought of going through a wedding again and actually becoming Prince Frederik's wife. She hesitantly turned her thoughts to an idea that she had been avoiding: Maybe she could run away... The Queen had to admit to herself that it was tempting.

"Here you go, Your Majesty," the boy chirped up before Dalia could entertain the "running away" idea any further.

She watched as the stable boy gripped the leather reins tied around a stunning, black horse. The muscles under his shining flank pulsed with strength and his dark eyes met her own unwaveringly. Staring at the tall beast, Dalia suddenly remembered the last time she had been out riding: It *had* been with Aeryn. This majestic colt had always been Aeryn's first pick of horses. That day, it had been hot and sticky outside, but the view of the pretty, green leaves surrounding them, and the soft grass squishing underneath their horses' hooves had been well worth it. During that ride, Aeryn had been trying to convince Dalia not to go through with the wedding.

"He is in *love* with *someone else*." Aeryn had spat out each word, accentuating them with an exasperated flip of her blonde hair, stringy and frizzy from the humidity.

Dalia couldn't precisely remember what her reply had been, but she probably said something about "duty." The Queen snorted and let out a slight chuckle. What had once been a duty to her, she was now running away from.

Dalia grabbed the reins from the boy's rough

hands. "Thank you."

She turned around to exit the stable, the horse following obediently behind her, but then she halted.

"Uh," she whispered over her shoulder to the stable boy, "please don't tell anyone you saw me."

# Chapter 4

Dalia smacked the reins against her horse's neck about a dozen times, urging him to go faster. Amazingly, he was able to comply. The chill wind stung her eyes, and she could feel water begin to pool within them. She shook the rest of the curls out as her hair flew in the wind behind her.

The trees' leaves shaded in the various reds and oranges of autumn flew out at her as she rode down the path. It was a path she had followed many times before, but she had never gone more than a few miles into the woods behind the castle. However, Dalia was planning on changing that today.

"I'm not running away," she whispered to herself. "I just… I just need time to think is all."

The Queen gripped the reins in her hands tightly as she attempted to allow her own words to console her. She ignored the leather biting at the flesh of her palms and continued onward. Soon the wide trail she followed narrowed, then shortly after that, it became non-existent. Dalia had officially reached further than she had ever gone before. She pushed on just a few minutes longer, determined to put a fair amount of distance between herself and whoever might have been sent after her.

Pulling the reins back as hard as she could, the horse came to a halt, hooves skidding against the grass. The ground was slick from rain that must have poured just hours before. Dalia swung her legs over the saddle, but before she could brave a leap off, she eyed the distance she was from the ground. The Queen was used to stable hands helping her on and off the royal steeds, but having to do it by herself made her shortness quite apparent to her.

Squinting her eyes shut and taking a deep breath, Dalia pushed herself off. As she landed, she felt her right ankle buckle underneath her weight. She hissed from the pain and collapsed on the ground, grabbing her foot and swaying back and forth.

"Ugh!" she cried.

Dalia dared a look at the injury and grimaced at the beginning signs of swelling. Biting her lip, she placed her arms behind her and began to push herself up into a standing position, but before she could do so, she heard a loud rustling to her left. Dalia whipped her head in the direction of the sound, eyes growing wide in fright. She held her breath and craned her neck to achieve a better view of what might be behind the foliage and tall, oak trees.

Slowly, a large, black paw emerged from behind the ferns and shrubs. A small whimper escaped from Dalia's lips. She scurried into a standing position, ignoring the biting pain shooting from her ankle and all the way through her leg. The rest of the bear's body appeared from its hiding place and entered the clearing. Dalia froze in place but noticed as her horse's ears perked up to the bear's footsteps. As soon as the steed saw the animal, it whinnied in fright and thrashed its head about. Within seconds, the palace horse turned and sprinted in the opposite direction of the bear.

Dalia could feel the blood leave her face as she watched the horse abandon her, then she slowly moved her attention back to the bear. The beast lifted itself onto its hind legs. Though maybe ten feet away, its shadow cast by the setting sun towered over Dalia's head. She gulped as she took in the sight of the monster. It was enormous, maybe seven feet tall as it stood before her, and at *least* a few hundred pounds. Its fur was dark as night, and its beady eyes were just as black. But Dalia didn't scream…

As the bear cocked its round head to the side and stared at her, unfazed by the horse running away, Dalia felt herself do the same. The two of them kept eye contact, studying one another curiously. Dalia could feel her nerves calming as the trembling in her limbs ceased. There was something different about this bear. It was almost as if it possessed some sort of intelligence— definitely more than any other animal she had ever come across.

Dalia took a deep breath and prepared herself to step forward but was interrupted by a sharp "Hush!" coming from behind her. Out of the corner of her eye, Dalia could see the form of a young man. Moving her head just enough to see the rest of him, she guessed him to be two or three years older than her eighteen years. He approached her slowly, right hand outstretched in a gesture to keep her quiet and left hand clinging to a worn hatchet.

"Don't move. Don't scream," he whispered.

"I wasn't going—"

The young man hushed her again, and Dalia bit down on her tongue in annoyance.

"The trick with bears," he continued in his low, gruff voice, "is to remain calm and let them know you're not a threat." He shifted his gaze to Dalia and looked her up and down with glowing, hazel eyes. "Or prey."

Dalia narrowed her eyes at him, almost forgetting the enormous bear standing before them. The young man sidestepped and put himself between the Queen and the bear. He didn't point the hatchet in his hand towards the animal, but Dalia could see the knuckles of his hands turning white as he held the weapon tightly in his grip, preparing to use it if he had to.

"Hey, bear," he said calmly. Dalia was surprised to see someone stand before a bear and keep his voice so steady. "We're not gonna hurt you."

The animal made a soft grunt and leaned forward to sniff the air in front of the young man. Dalia could see the man's muscles tense underneath his worn, brown cloak as he shifted the wooden bow and small sheath of arrows hanging atop his broad shoulders.

"I don't think he's going to hurt us," Dalia volunteered as she studied the way the bear was interacting with the two of them. The animal responded to the sound of her voice, looking in her direction and opening his muzzle to reveal its yellow, jagged teeth. It looked almost like a... smile.

The stranger lowered his right arm slowly and cocked his head to the side, which caused his brown hair that grew to just above his shoulders to all fall over to one side.

"Interesting..." he breathed, stepping back to stand beside the Queen.

Dalia allowed herself a quick glance at his features. He was lean and fit, and a slight shadow of hair was growing on his tan cheeks, which accentuated the fatigued look in his eyes. Though tired and ragged, she could tell he was still a handsome man. Dalia felt her face grow hot, ashamed of herself for thinking such things when face-to-face with a bear — even if it *wasn't* going to attack them.

The three of them stood quietly in the clearing, and the only sounds passing were distant chirpings of various birds and the wind rustling the leaves in the trees. Dalia and the strange man didn't dare move as the bear studied the two of them, even as it moved from its hind legs to a relaxed, sitting position. Seconds turned to minutes, and soon the sun had set entirely over the horizon.

"How long do you think we have to stay like this?" Dalia muttered out the side of her mouth, barely moving her dry lips. She licked at them slightly, trying to remember the last time she had something to drink.

Before the young man could reply, the bear heaved itself back onto its four paws with a loud grunt, which sounded awfully close to a heavy sigh. Then, it turned around and trotted back in the direction from where it had come.

Dalia and the stranger let out a long breath of air simultaneously, both overcome with relief.

"Good thing I came when I did!" the young man exclaimed, sheathing the hatchet's dull blade at his side.

Dalia shoved her fists on her narrow hips. "I was *fine*!"

He raised an eyebrow and looked down at her, making Dalia feel very aware of their stark differences in height, but she stayed her ground.

"Really," she insisted.

The stranger chuckled and shook his head, obviously not believing her. Before Dalia could protest any further, her brain suddenly registered the pain radiating from her injured ankle. She shouted out and crumbled underneath her weight to the forest floor.

"What in the world?"

"It's my ankle!" she hissed through her teeth. "I hurt it right before... right before..."

"Let me take a look." He threw his tattered cloak behind himself and knelt beside her. He quickly pulled off his leather gloves, then reached for her foot.

Dalia protectively grabbed her leg and pulled away from him. He sat back on his heels and pursed his lips.

"I just want to help," he said.

Dalia hesitated a moment, but then relented and allowed him to take her foot into his callused hands. The young man gingerly pulled off her boot but stopped as he caught sight of the woven, satin sock covering her foot. She felt her heart stop. Only nobles owned such luxury in clothing. Dalia didn't want him to know she was the Queen— in fear he would insist on taking her back to the castle or maybe even kidnap her for ransom.

The young man opened and closed his mouth to say something, but seemed to change his mind as he shook his head and slid the sock off.

"I'm Nicholas Smith, by the way," he said as he began rolling her ankle back and forth to test it. Dalia bit her lip and curled her toes against the pain as he moved it.

"Does that hurt?"

"Just a little," she lied.

Nicholas gingerly rolled the sock back over her toes and past her swollen ankle. "I don't think it's broken," he said. "But it is a pretty bad sprain." He craned his neck up to the darkening sky and the twinkling of stars beginning to peek out from hiding. "I don't think you should be traveling anymore tonight." Nicholas eyed her curiously. "Where *were* you headed, exactly? All alone and so late, might I add?"

Dalia gulped. "I was just going for a ride, but my horse ran away once it saw the bear." It was the truth. Granted, she left out a few important details, like her royal lineage, but what he didn't know wouldn't hurt him.

Nicholas furrowed his thick brows and looked as if he wished to say more, but he shrugged it off. He stood up with a slight groan and brushed off the few blades of grass and specks of dirt sticking to his clothing.

"Well, we should get you somewhere safe for the night. Do you mind if I carry you?"

The Queen stiffened, thinking through all of the worst-case scenarios that could happen when heading deep into the woods with a man she had never met, but she concluded that she had no choice. For one thing, no one from the castle had found her yet, and the lack of a horse and a new injury made it nearly impossible to travel back on her own. She raised her arms in compliance as Nicholas reached down to lift her into his grasp. He held her tight against his chest and began heading in the opposite direction the bear had set off to. Dalia couldn't help but notice the pleasant, woodsy smell coming from him. It was also warm in his strong arms, and she had to fight off the desire to nuzzle into his oddly comforting touch.

"You haven't told me your name yet," Nicholas said as he angled himself through a narrow passage between two trees.

"Oh!" Dalia placed her fingers on her cheeks as another flush crept up her face. "Um, I'm…"

"Do you not know your own name?"

"Of course I know it. It's Aeryn Parcell." Dalia caught her breath as she heard her friend's name escape her lips. She hadn't even thought it through before blurting it out, but she didn't want this stranger to know she was the Queen, either.

"What brings you out here, Nicholas?" she said, trying to distract him from her red face.

She shifted in his grip as he shrugged. "I'm a huntsman. Spending a lot of time in the woods is kind of my thing. And please, just call me Nick."

There was a long pause, and it was completely silent except for the sound of fallen leaves crushing underneath Nick's boots.

"Now, I must ask you again: why are *you* out here?"

Dalia winced, wondering if her asking him a similar question earlier guided him into directing it to her once again, but she then realized he was bound to be curious about a young woman traveling by herself anyway.

"I was out for a ride, but my horse was spooked by the bear and ran away." She was feeling annoyed by the redundancy of having to explain herself to him.

"I've been running into a lot of strange girls in the woods lately," Nick breathed, growing slightly tired from trudging so long with the Queen in his arms.

Dalia was surprised the huntsman didn't push her for more of an answer, but upon further examination of the grim look on his face, she could tell his mind was on something else.

"A *lot* of strange girls? I'm not the only one?"

Nick clenched his jaw, and a shadow flashed across his face, making the angles in his cheeks look hollow and sickly. Dalia wondered how long it had been since the young man had a decent meal.

After a good while with no answer from the mysterious huntsman, she decided not to press the issue and changed the subject:

"Where are you taking me?"

Nick chuckled at an inward joke. Dalia raised an eyebrow, a movement he could not see due to their positioning.

"Nowhere in particular," he said. "I'm not one to settle down any place. Especially recently."

The silence grew stark once again as Nick seemed to return to those same thoughts that had saddened him before, but Dalia ignored it this time. Craning her neck past Nick's arms, the Queen stared back in the direction they had come. They were growing further and further away from the castle, the place she would typically call her home. But lately, it had been feeling more like a prison.

Dalia continued to keep her eyes on the path behind them, trying to decide whether the thrill she felt from leaving that life behind, even for as short a time it may be, was a good thing.

# Chapter 5

Dalia dreamt of the magical looking glass, with its illusion of swirling smoke and flashing lights. But instead of revealing what she had asked for— a view of the roaring, blue oceans of Wilaldan— the mirror faded into an image of Prince Frederik. He stood in the throne room, dressed in his wedding garb and looking regal as ever. His frosty eyes locked onto hers and glowed simultaneously with kindness and eagerness as he outstretched his hand towards Dalia.

"No," she whispered.

Suddenly, darkness replaced the smile on the Prince's handsome face. Glowering, he leapt forward, and his arms slid through the glass as if it was liquid. Dalia cried out and dropped the mirror, but Frederik's strong hands wrapped around her neck and squeezed before it could hit the floor. The mirror seemed to hang from his elbows as the rest of his body still remained in the glass.

"Please," Dalia choked.

He was trying to pull her in— back to him, back to their wedding, back to her life, back to... Being Queen.

All of a sudden, everything disappeared: the mirror, the Prince... And she stood alone in blackness.

"I can't do it!" she screamed to nothing. "I don't want to do it anymore!"

Dalia woke with a start and smacked her head against the wide trunk of a tree. She yelped in pain and began to rub the back of her head. Blinking, her sight began to clear, and Dalia was able to remember where she was.

Dalia propped herself up, feeling the damp soil of the forest floor begin to dirty her palms. A small fire was burning just a few feet from where she sat, and in front of it was Nick. He sat with his back against a rotting tree, hatchet in one hand, and a whetstone in the other. The sound of metal against stone set Dalia's teeth on edge. She squinted her eyes to get a better look at the huntsman over the fire. It wasn't quite dawn, so it was still a bit dark, and the fire was casting so many shadows that it was hard for Dalia to read the expression on his face.

"Bad dream?"

Dalia drew her brows together. "How did you know?"

Nick let out a short chortle. "You were screaming, 'I can't do it! I don't want to do it anymore!'" The huntsman glanced up from his hatchet and leaned forward, the flames of the fire reflecting off his eyes playfully. "What do you not want to do anymore, Aeryn?"

Dalia winced at his use of the name "Aeryn," suddenly remembering that she had given him a false name. "I don't remember," she lied.

Nick raised a thick eyebrow. Dalia knew he didn't believe her. She shifted uncomfortably under his gaze, but soon he shrugged and went back to sharpening his weapon.

The Queen let out a soft sigh in relief and rested her head back onto the hard ground, but any feelings of ease quickly went away as her thoughts returned to the dream. Dalia definitely knew what that nightmare had been about, but she had been avoiding even *thinking* about it for so long. Her stomach churned as she remembered the feeling of walking down the aisle to wed Prince Frederik. But it wasn't just that... Ever since Dalia had become Queen, she hadn't been happy. She despised ruling, especially since no one ever let her actually rule. Everyone, not just Lady Violetta, seemed to treat her like a daft child.

Dalia stared at the sky as it slowly turned into a light blue as the sun began to peek out on the horizon. She had only been away from the castle for less than a day, but she was already feeling more relaxed than she had in ages— even after an encounter with a bear and a strange huntsman. She knew she couldn't stay away forever, but Dalia wondered about the possibilities of attaining more than just a *little* taste of freedom; She wanted something permanent.

"Don't be ridiculous," she muttered to herself with a shake of her head.

"Did you say something?" Nick inquired without taking the time to look in her direction.

Dalia studied the young man across from her and found herself wishing she could confide in him. She used to have that with Aeryn, the *real* Aeryn, but there was no way of knowing if she could trust Nick.

And yet, he had helped her thus far and hadn't tried anything questionable the entire night and through part of the morning. He just sat against a tree going about his own business. But she couldn't risk letting him in on her identity; His motives could very well change when obtaining the knowledge that he was in the presence of royalty.

The sound of horses' hooves reached Dalia's ears as they crunched dead leaves on the ground.

"Oh no!" she squeaked, scrambling off the grass and leaping up onto her feet. "They found me!"

Nick jumped, startled. "*Who* found you?" He whipped his head back and forth. "I hear horses. They don't sound too far off."

Dalia squinted her eyes shut and resisted the urge to smack her palm against her forehead. Now there was *no* possibility of keeping her identity secret. But she couldn't think of that now.

"Please," she whispered frantically. "I don't want them to find me."

Nick responded only with a blank look.

"I'll explain later!" she snapped.

The huntsman hesitantly rose from his position, but still walked over to the Queen and outstretched his hand.

"Come on," he whispered. "Let's hide you."

Dalia took his callused hand in hers and lifted up

her grass-stained skirts with the other to catch up with Nick's long strides.

He led her to a thick line of bushes. Pulling them back, Nick revealed a shallow ditch among the roots.

"Lie down there." He let go of her hand and gestured to the ground.

Taking a deep breath, Dalia reluctantly complied and slid into the hole. She yelped as bits of twigs and small rocks poked into her skin.

"You have to be *really* quiet," he warned.

Dalia began shaking, but she nodded.

The clopping sound of the horses' hooves grew closer. Dalia pressed her hand tightly against her mouth and nose to quiet her breathing. Her palm smelled of dirt, but that was the last thing on her mind.

She could hear the landing of two heavy feet on the forest floor as someone dismounted their steed. Dalia stretched her neck out to dare a peek, but all she could see through the foliage were the dark, leather boots of the newcomer, and the legs of three horses shifting about restlessly.

"Tell me, huntsman. Have you seen the Queen come by?" The voice was deep and rumbled through the ground and to Dalia's ears. She didn't recognize the man's voice, but she had so many servants, it was hard to keep track.

"The *Queen*?" Nick guffawed loudly. "You can't be serious! Alone in the woods?"

Dalia winced. He was bound to figure it out sooner or later.

There was a long pause, and Dalia wished she could see the man's reaction. Soon, the silence grew uncomfortable. She began pleading silently for the conversation to continue, then end, allowing the men searching for her to be on their way. Her breath began to grow hot behind her hand, so she cracked open a couple fingers to inhale some fresh air.

"Yes, the Queen." There was a hint of annoyance in the man's voice. It was as if he understood the ridiculousness of the situation. "She has... disappeared."

The man most likely didn't want to advertise that their ruler ran away from not only her own wedding but also her responsibilities as the monarch. That fact sent a pang through Dalia's heart and made her feel guilty. The man continued:

"We have reason to believe she went for a ride in these woods yesterday."

Dalia could see Nick's foot bouncing up and down. "What does she look like?" he asked. "I saw her once, but that was a long time ago and from a distance." He paused, and Dalia could see his frame shift slightly in her direction as he thought. "At least I *think* it was only once."

The servant chuckled slightly. "You can't miss her. Her Majesty's red hair sticks out like a sore thumb."

Dalia grit her teeth as she saw Nick freeze. She could picture his jaw growing tight, and his eyes narrowing. How was he going to react? How was he going to feel about her lying to him? She awaited the words that would give her away, but the huntsman surprised her:

"Nope. Haven't seen her."

The Queen bit her tongue so hard to suppress a gasp that it began to bleed. That had not been what she expected. Maybe she could trust Nick after all. Unless he had an ulterior motive, but she couldn't begin to guess what such a motive might even be.

"Hm." The man sounded unconvinced. "Well, keep a sharp eye out, will you?"

"Of course!" Nick responded.

Dalia slowly scooted herself slightly closer to the ditch's edge to better reach a view of the man. She could now see above his boots, but she still couldn't see much above his knees. He turned around and dug his foot into one of the stirrups strapped to his horse, then heaved himself up onto the saddle with a deep grunt. He clicked his tongue, and his steed began trotting away, the man's two companions following suit with their own animals.

Dalia continued to hold her breath and waited for Nick to tell her it was safe to emerge. After a couple of minutes, the huntsman turned quickly on his heel and stomped in the Queen's direction. He knelt down beside the ditch and poked his head through the greenery she was hiding behind.

"You have some explaining to do, Your Majesty."

# Chapter 6

Nick was angry with her, but Dalia couldn't completely understand why. He acted as if he had been betrayed and kept muttering to himself about needing to stop helping strange women he found wandering in the woods. He paced back and forth across the clearing they had slept in the night before. He was even wearing down the dry grass beneath his feet.

It was actually kind of refreshing for Dalia to see someone annoyed with her— someone that wasn't the Lady Violetta. Most people would have learned of her identity and immediately made sure they did everything in their power to please her. But not Nick. He was frustrated with her lies and secrecy. However, he definitely seemed to be overreacting.

"Why is it such a big deal?" Dalia finally said. "I just wanted to be away from the castle for a while, and I didn't want anyone to know who I was." Her eyes lowered to the ground, and her voice grew softer: "It was actually quite invigorating not to be the Queen for a bit."

"It's a big deal because—" Nick stopped pacing and rubbed his face with his hands. "I'm sorry. I'm taking out my anger with someone else on you." He glanced at Dalia sheepishly. "It's a long story."

Dalia opened her mouth to push him on the subject, but he interjected:

"I'm starving. We need to catch something for breakfast. We should also probably start moving away from this area. Especially if you don't want those men to find you, *my Queen*."

The way he said those last two words made Dalia flinch. It definitely didn't seem like Nick was moving past things like he appeared to be intending when offering breakfast.

Before she could even blink, Nick had already begun trotting off deep into the woods, making sure to go in the opposite direction of the castle men.

"Wait for me!" she hollered, yanking up her skirts and sprinting after him.

Dalia groaned as she remembered her injured ankle, but pushed past the throbbing pain to catch up to Nick. The morning dew on the blades of grass made the dirt wet and squished as she walked. Finally, she caught up to him, and Nick was crouching down within a tall patch of grass. He squatted on the balls of his feet and had pulled his large bow off of his shoulders.

"What are you doing?"

"Hush!" he hissed at her, waving at her with annoyance. "There's a squirrel over there."

Dalia grimaced. "Squirrel? To *eat*?"

The huntsman shot her a fiery look and gestured for her to crouch down. He then moved his attention back to the animal. It took Dalia a bit of time to find it, but after searching the thick line of oak trees, she saw it: The squirrel had a nut in his hand about twice the size of its own fists. The thick patch of gray fur around its little neck bounced up and down as it gnawed on its food.

"It looks a little too scrawny to provide a substantial meal."

Nick palmed his face softly. "Your Majesty, will you *please* be quiet. We don't want to scare it off."

Dalia wanted to protest and point out that her whisper had been remarkably quiet, but she bit down on her tongue to stop herself. However, his insolence was getting slightly more frustrating than it had been earlier.

"Sorry," she mouthed to him, but he either didn't notice or ignored her.

Nick leaned forward and pulled out his bow in front of him. Dalia noticed the splinters all along its side and scrunched up her nose as she saw one slip into his index finger, but he didn't even flinch. Slowly, he pulled a slim arrow out of his quiver and slid it into the drawstring. He squinted his eyes tightly, the irises adopting more of a brown hazel color than green as he pulled the drawstring to his cheek. Dalia could see the muscles in his arms tighten as he stretched the bow. Blowing out a deep breath, his fingers poised to release the arrow, but a loud shout from the distance erupted.

Nick jumped, startled, and the drawstring flew out of Nick's fingers with a twang and smacked the inside of his left arm.

"Ouch!" he cried out, grabbing at his arm with the uninjured one.

Dalia watched in fear as the arrow flew but couldn't quite catch where it landed. But it definitely didn't land anywhere *near* their breakfast. The tiny squirrel nearly jumped out of its skin at the commotion and scurried away into the treetops.

Nick let out a frustrated groan and punched at the ground with his uninjured arm. Before either one could say anything, the unknown person continued to holler out loudly.

"Help! Is anyone out there?" The distressed voice sounded male.

Dalia and Nick exchanged confused glances, then leapt up from the ground and ran towards the shouting. Thankfully, the shouting came from a direction nowhere near where the men from the castle had ridden off to. Dalia was pleased to find that her ankle was beginning to feel better. It only brought about a dull ache as she ran. Maybe it just needed to be walked on a bit.

The wind whistled in her ears as Dalia ran and felt bitter cold against her cheeks. However, Nick didn't seem to mind as he kept his eyes wide open and didn't falter in his stride.

"If there is someone out there ignoring me, I *swear* you will meet my wrath!" the scratchy, gruff voice bellowed.

Dalia halted for a moment at the threats, then couldn't help but let out a snicker. Nick slowed down.

"Come on!" he said, grabbing her arm, but she could see a small smile on his lips, as well.

They reached the shouting man after about a minute, but they both stopped in their tracks as they beheld the scene before them. No more than four feet tall, a little man stood directly in front of a tree and was yanking at his white beard. The beard was dirtied from about a dozen patches of dirt, which made it look browner than its normal color. The beard protruding from the man's wrinkled face was about as long as he was short. Dalia moved her eyes slowly to the end of its trail and noticed a good chunk of hair wrapped within a gaping hole in the chipping wood and sticking to bits of twigs and rocks stuck inside it. He looked ridiculous, and it didn't help that he wore what looked almost like a potato sack with matching trousers

The man turned his head to Dalia and Nick, cheeks red and dark eyes fuming.

"Don't just stand there!" he snapped. "Pull me out of here!"

Dalia almost couldn't process his words as she stared at the bushy eyebrows resting on his thick forehead. They grew out practically down to his cheekbones.

"Sorry! Of course." Nick's reply to the angry man shook Dalia out of her amazed stupor, and she moved with the huntsman to assist.

Nick towered over the little man as he stood next to the tree, studying the situation. Dalia's initial impression of the huntsman had been that he was very tall, but compared to the bearded man, he was a giant!

"Maybe all three of us should pull it," Dalia offered.

"No!" the man cried, frantically shifting his eyes about. "That'll be *much* too painful. Try untangling it."

Nick reached down towards the hole in the trunk and twisted his fingers around the hairs in an attempt to free the beard. The space was too small for all three of them to fit, so Dalia stood on the tips of her toes to get a good look at what was going on.

"It's pretty stuck," Nick said with a grunt as he pulled himself out. His thick, brown bangs fell into his face as he stepped back. He shoved his hands on his hips and pursed his lips. "I think we have to cut it out."

The man's eyes grew as big as saucers. He flew his head back and forth between the two.

"I think he's right," Dalia agreed.

The stranger's chapped, bottom lip began to quiver. "No, no, no, no, *no*! It took me so long to get my beard this voluminous and soft. Not to mention its length! And did you see my perfect eyebrows?"

Dalia bit her lip and trembled from trying to keep a laugh from escaping her lips, but she wasn't very successful. The man squinted her eyes at her.

"What's so funny, child?" he growled. "My beautiful hair is much better than that red eyesore swinging from your head.

Nick threw his head back and laughed. "I bet you're not used to someone talking to you like that, huh?" he directed to the Queen.

Dalia felt her face grow hot and shifted her eyes downward.

'What's that supposed to mean?" the dwarf spat. "You're sweetheart there doesn't hold a candle to our kind. They have gorgeous beards, bright eyes, are occasionally stronger than us men—"

Nick shook his head emphatically and took two steps away from Dalia. "She's not my sweetheart."

But Dalia hadn't heard the "sweetheart" part of the man's monologue. Her mind remained on the other things he said.

"Your women have *beards*? And what do you mean by *your* kind?" she probed.

"I'm a dwarf, you idiot."

Dalia gasped, and Nick merely chuckled.

"If only he knew who he was talking to," Nick giggled while wiping a tear from his eye.

Both Dalia and the so-called "dwarf" ignored him. "Dwarves don't exist!" she said.

"Oh, they do," Nick and the dwarf said simultaneously.

Dalia whirled around on the huntsman. "How do you know?"

He shrugged. "I lived with seven of them for a little while."

"You lived with *seven dwarves*?" she jeered with a chuckle. "You can't be serious."

"Actually, they were *half*-dwarves," he added while holding up his finger matter-of-factly.

Before Dalia could even begin to muster up a reply,

the dwarf chimed in:

"Hey! You must be talking about my seven nephews! They are why I am here in Edristan, actually. I am one of their many uncles. I traveled all the way from Lurid to pick them up." The dwarf clicked his tongue. "Sad what they've been through."

Nick lowered his head and nodded solemnly. Dalia merely raised an eyebrow and held out her arms, exasperated. No one ever seemed to want to explain anything to her.

"I'm Aephrys, by the way."

"Nick. And this is…" He paused, narrowing his eyes at the Queen. Dalia knew that Nick had was debating on whether or not to tell the dwarf her true identity.

"This is Aeryn," he decided to say.

Dalia sighed in relief and attempted to shoot a grateful look in Nick's direction, but he avoided her gaze.

"Anyway!" the dwarf barked, completely changing his attitude once again. "Let's get me out of this tree."

# Chapter 7

Aephrys sat on the forest floor with his stubby fingers running through his knotted beard. Giant teardrops streamed down his face and disappeared into his whiskers as he continued to mourn his lost facial hair.

"It took me *centuries* to get it to that length," he moaned.

Centuries? Dalia rolled her eyes. First an enchanted mirror, then some poisoned apples, and now this? It was like she lived in one of those fairy-tale stories her father used to read her when she was a child.

"I only chopped off two or three inches," Nick retorted while wiping away the stringy, white beard hairs off of his hatchet. "It'll grow back."

Before the dwarf could reply, a loud grunt and heavy shuffling sounded from behind the distant trees.

"What was that?" Dalia breathed, frightened to think the men had found her already.

Aephrys leapt up from the ground and whirled towards the noise excitedly. "Charles? Is that you?"

It emerged after a bit more rustling: The big, black bear from before clumped its way out of hiding.

"Charles!" the dwarf cried, rushing to the animal.

Nick and Dalia exchanged glances, both still tense and stiff in apprehension. They watched as Aephrys dug himself into the thick coat of fur and nuzzled the bear.

"I thought I lost you!" he gushed. The bear playfully pawed at the dwarf's little head, looking just as excited as Aephrys.

"Uh, you know the… the bear?" Nick asked wearily.

"He's my pet!" Aephrys declared.

Dalia felt herself relax and let out a laugh. "You said you came from Lurid, right? That's an entirely separate continent from the five kingdoms! How did you bring over a *bear*?"

The dwarf stopped wrestling with the bear and placed his hands on his hips firmly. He pursed his lips at Nick and Dalia.

"I have my own boat, you know."

Dalia suppressed an eye roll. "Oh, of course," she replied, yet still unsatisfied with his explanation.

"I guess that explains why the bear didn't attack us earlier," Nick said, feeling comfortable enough to sheath his hatchet.

Aephrys's jaw dropped. "You saw him? When? Why didn't you tell me?"

Nick held up his hands defensively. "Whoa, how were we supposed to know it was *your* bear?"

The dwarf's glare was so hot, Dalia was surprised it didn't burn a hole through the huntsman. "Charles is not an 'it,'" he spat. "Charles is a 'he.'"

Nick didn't reply initially, trying to give Aephrys a chance to respond to his initial question, but the dwarf went right back to playing with his pet.

"*He*. Sorry," Nick said with a slight eye roll.

Dalia snickered slightly, and Nick followed suit. Soon, both fell into a fit of laughter with each other.

Aephrys turned his attention away from the bear once again. "What? What's so funny?"

Dalia wiped tears away from her eyes as she continued to laugh. "I think it's just been a strange, long couple of days for the two of us.

"Definitely," Nick added. "But it's getting better now."

He flashed her a handsome smile, and the Queen could see the frustration he had been harboring for her disappear. Her heart skipped a beat. Suddenly seeing this playful, warm side of Nick was appealing to her. Dalia smiled back at him and felt a sense of relief wash over her as their shared laughter brought about reconcilement.

# Chapter 8

"Tell the boys I said 'hi!'" Nick called out as the dwarf hobbled away with Charles the bear at his side. The picture of the two of them was amusing; Their stark difference in sizes alone was enough to gawk and snicker at.

After they watched Aephrys disappear through the trees of the forest, Nick turned to Dalia with a frown.

"Look, I'm really sorry I was so angry with you, Your Majesty," he said.

Dalia waved his words away. "Please, call me Dalia. And I shouldn't be hiding my identity. I just thought something bad might happen if I told a stranger I was the Queen, but..." She studied Nick up and down, warmly remembering the moment they had shared just minutes before. "But I think I can trust you," she finished.

Nick smiled. "You can. I have no desire to harm you."

Dalia looked over her shoulder in the direction of the castle. At least, the direction she *thought* the castle was in. She was not very adept to the outdoors and directions. "I think it's time for me to go back."

She tilted her head back to squint up at the sky.

The sun's high position suggested it was already noon. Dalia had been gone for more than half a day. Her stomach churned to think about how worried everybody must be.

Nick furrowed his brow. "Why? Just a few hours ago, you were hiding away from the people sent to look for you."

Dalia lowered her head, the ache in her stomach growing stronger from guilt. "I have too many responsibilities that I shouldn't have run away from."

As she said it, she began to remember why she had agreed to marry Prince Frederik in the first place— for the good of her kingdom. But not only had she fled from her wedding, but Dalia also felt as if she had abandoned the people of Edristan.

Without noticing the onset of tears, it was too late for Dalia to stop them as they quickly spilled over her cheeks. She raised her fingers to her face to obscure them from the huntsman. However, Nick saw them and instinctively rushed to her side and put a strong arm around her shoulder. Dalia froze at his touch, feeling her face begin to grow warm, but soon relaxed and leaned into his shoulder.

They stood like that for a few seconds, but then both grew slightly uncomfortable and parted from one another. Nick cleared his throat, lowering his eyes to the ground, and Dalia began twirling a bit of red hair on her finger.

"I can help you get back," he finally said. "Of course, only if you want me to."

Dalia laughed. "I think I'll need all the help I can

get. I'm not used to being out in the woods for so long with no horse."

Nick chuckled and shook his head at Dalia. "I still can't believe I am talking with the *Queen*!" He then flushed slightly and shoved his hands in the pockets of his trousers. "I guess I just got upset with the lie because of an experience I had recently with another young woman." He shook his head and forced out a laugh. "It's kind of embarrassing, actually."

Dalia moved to rest a comforting hand on his arm but hesitated. With a subtle shake of her head and a bit of internal convincing, she finally did so. He relaxed and flashed her an appreciative smile

"It was foolish of me," he said. "I met this girl— a *beautiful* girl— in the woods. Kind of like how we met."

"Are you calling me beautiful, too?" Dalia joked.

"Sure," Nick said with a wink, which made Dalia's heart flutter. However, the feeling scared her, and she quickly let go of his arm, but it didn't seem to deter the huntsman.

"But I met this particular girl in a different set of woods," he continued. "It was pretty far from here, but we were still in Edristan." He took a deep breath. "Anyway, she seemed kind and just as beautiful in her heart as she was physically, but... she started to change. Or maybe she had *always* been like that, I don't know."

He shook his head emphatically and began clenching and unclenching his fists. Dalia cocked her head to the side and watched as Nick seemed to

have an internal battle with himself. He kept looking over at the Queen and opening his mouth to say
something, then changing his mind over and over
again.

"What is it?" Dalia asked. "You can tell me. I won't
throw you in the dungeon, I promise." She chuckled,
but Nick still looked grim. "Nick?"

"She was obsessed with you for some reason, Your
Majesty. She desperately wanted what you had."

Dalia narrowed her eyes. "What do you mean?"

"Your Prince. I think she was in love with him."

Dalia's heart stopped. "No," she breathed. "You
can't mean... Snow White?"

Nick stumbled, surprised as Dalia said the girl's
name. "So, you *do* know her."

Dalia blinked repeatedly, too shocked to answer,
but before she could begin speaking, a stream of
dark, tall horses cascaded into the area with loud
whinnies and hooves pounding against the earth.
Dalia stumbled from fright as the animals circled
around them, but Nick reached around the small of
her back to support her. He then grabbed her arms
and slid himself in front of the Queen, standing
protectively with his hands poised to reach for his
hatchet and bow.

There were definitely more horses and men in
this group than the first that had approached Nick
that morning. And all of their horses were various
shades of black instead of the lighter-colored ones
from earlier, as well.

The one directly in the center of the party had

the tallest horse, even among the larger than average size of the others. With narrowed, beady eyes, the man surveilled the two before him. Once his eyes saw the bushy, red hair revealing itself from behind Nick's back, the old man's chapped lips twisted into an unappealing smirk.

"Queen Dalia Char!" he shrilled in his piercing, high voice that didn't quite match the dark and robust look about him. "We have been looking for you."

# Chapter 9

"Who are you?" Nick demanded, continuing to hold Dalia back and behind him.

Dalia was so close to Nick that her cheek pressed up against his quiver of arrows. She winced as the woven material scratched against her skin. Still, she felt comforted by the protection of the huntsman, so she didn't dare move.

The older man in the center, who seemed to be the group leader, merely grinned and stepped in closer to the two of them. Nick inched himself and the Queen further away, but they were trapped in on the other side, as well.

"We heard the young Queen ran off from her wedding and hadn't been seen for a little while," he answered, leaning over to his side to get a good view of Dalia and winking at her. "We're here to take her."

Dalia felt Nick's fingers tighten around her arm.

"Back to the castle?" he asked.

An eruption of laughter sounded around them. Dalia darted her eyes around and at the men surrounding them— each met her gaze with sly grins on their wiry and scruffy faces. She shuddered underneath their stares.

"No," the leader snickered. "We're here to kidnap

her."

Dalia's heart dropped to her stomach with a thud, and she felt her limbs grow stiff. But Nick was quick to react: He pulled his hatchet out of its sheath in one swift, fluid motion, which only made the men continue in their laughter. Dalia eyed the various swords and daggers at their hips and in their hands. Nick's little ax looked pathetic next to the weapons they wielded.

"I won't let you!" Nick shouted over the hooting and amused chatter.

The old man raised an amused eyebrow and drew his own rapier from his side. The sword was thin and short, but could definitely hold up in a fight against a dull, overused hatchet.

"Then I'll just have to kill you." But even as the man said it, his grip on the sword loosened as if he was feeling hesitant, but Dalia didn't want to take any chances.

"No!" Dalia cried, shoving herself in front of Nick. "Please don't hurt him."

"Dalia," Nick hissed, "don't."

"Look at that, men! The little girl is trying to be brave!" The man looked Dalia up and down, then turned his nose into the air. His hesitation and slight nervousness from before seemed to disappear just as quickly as it had come. "How adorable."

Dalia knew she should feel scared, but as the man jeered at her and the others laughed, she felt a burning fury build up inside her.

"How *dare* you!" she fumed. "I am still your

Queen!" She squared her shoulders back and took two steps forward. "There are people out here looking for me, and I am sure they are not far. You *will* be found, and I will make sure each and every single one of you is punished for your crimes." She took her turn to eye the leader up and down and sneer at him. "Crimes of which, I'm sure, are many in number."

"Oooh," the leader goaded, urging the rest of his crew to chime in with a wave of his arms. "You have us *so* frightened, Your Majesty. Look at me!" The man began shaking his short legs. "I have become wobbly in the knees!"

Dalia clenched her fists but slightly relaxed as Nick came up beside her and took one of her hands in his.

"Take the Queen," the leader directed one of the men astride a horse on his left. And to the one on his right, he said, "And the little boy, too. I don't feel like making a mess right now."

Nick's face grew dark as he clenched his jaw. "Little boy?" he growled through his teeth. Dalia yelped slightly as his grip on her hand tightened.

The two men directed to grab Nick and Dalia dismounted their horses. They approached with grubby hands outstretched and vile smirks plastered onto their faces.

Dalia studied them closely. The one on the left was scrawny and sickly and could easily be overtaken by the huntsman and herself, but the one on the right towered over even Nick by at least a foot and was quite stocky in build. He could grab both of them in his grasp with little effort. Not to mention the other men that could come to their aid, if need be.

"What are we going to do?" Dalia whispered to Nick as the two men continued to close in on them.

Nick flexed his fingers that held the hatchet in his left hand and poised the other arm to pull off his bow. But as he studied the situation before him, the huntsman soon faltered in his stance, shoulders falling and eyes moving to ground.

"I don't know, Dalia." He looked over at her, frown setting deeply into his face. "I don't know.

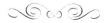

Aephrys whistled happily as he and Charles strolled under the colorful leaves. He breathed in the crisp air deeply through his nose and chuckled as the few warm rays of the sun penetrated through the treetops and to his face. He was in a much better mood now than he had been when stuck in that tree. And also now that he had been reunited with his beloved pet.

Aephrys glanced over at his bear and beamed under his bushy beard. "I thought I had lost you, Charles."

The bear lifted his long snout in the air, opened his muzzle wide, and let out a loud and happy grunt. Aephrys playfully nudged Charles with his shoulder, which didn't deter the bear from his walking what-soever due to their extreme difference in size and weight.

Aephrys liked having a bear almost twice his height and at least four times as heavy as he for pro-tection— especially in a land where the dwarf had no understanding of the people and the culture. And so far, the Kingdom of Edristan was *very* different from the secluded caves Aephrys lived in with the other dwarves high in Lurid's mountains. For one thing, Edristan was crawling with an overpopula-tion of imbecilic, ugly humans.

Aephrys shook his head as they walked. He never had been able to understand humankind, with their stomping about, clean faces, ridiculous parties, al-ways wanting to talk to each other... If Aephrys could have it his way, he would be deep within a mountain hammering away at stone and sitting in the heaps of precious diamonds he and his brothers would find in just one day. Of course, he was grateful for that huntsman and his woman companion for coming to his aid earlier. Even if they *did* cut his pre-cious beard.

The dwarf began stroking the facial hair, wrap-ping the length of it around his arm fondly, then scowling at the uneven chopping at the bottom. He would have to get his beard trimmed and groomed when he got back home with those nephews of his.

Aephrys frowned to himself as he thought of the seven boys. When their brother Udril had gone off and married that human, Aephrys and the others had felt betrayed and ashamed. But a large part of him felt guilty for never trying to reconcile with Udril before his untimely death. Aephrys kept a small bit of hope burning within him that retrieving his late brother's sons could be his own way of making up for that. He just had to try and get over the boys' half-human lineage.

Aephrys suddenly stopped in his tracks and palmed his thick forehead.

"Charles!" he cried. "I don't know where those poor boys live, and we were *just* with someone who *did* know!" He shook his head emphatically, almost inclined to laugh at himself, but feeling too grumpy to allow it. "And the chances of finding a person with that knowledge were very slim, to begin with. I can't believe I didn't ask!" Aephrys tugged on the dark scruff of the bear's neck to turn him around. "We better go back before they leave, and we can't find them."

Charles began galavanting through the dead grass, the piles of fallen leaves crushing completely underneath his heavy footfalls. Aephrys scurried his little legs after him, but to no avail.

"Wait!" he cried. "Charles! You *know* I'm not fast!"

The bear skidded to a halt and flung his head behind his shoulder and looked at Aephrys with big, mopey eyes.

"Oh, don't you go looking all innocent."

The bear waddled back as Aephrys tapped his foot impatiently. Once reaching the dwarf, Charles crouched down to his level, offering the little man to climb atop his back. Aephrys rolled his eyes and groaned.

"You know how much I detest riding you. It makes me feel even smaller, and you smell *terrible*. However…" The dwarf looked ahead in the direction where they had left the huntsman and his companion. "I guess my short legs aren't going to do much in trying to catch up with them, huh?"

After taking a deep breath and releasing it heavily through his nose, Aephrys scrambled onto his pet with great effort. It took longer than he liked as it was hard to keep his footing and had to climb a good amount due to his height— he was even shorter than average for a *dwarf*. He was just glad no one was watching his embarrassing attempts at mounting a bear.

"Heigh, ho!" he shouted, kicking Charles's flank.

The bear looked up at him, big eyes narrowed as if offended by the dwarf treating him like a horse. Aephrys held up his arms defensively.

"Hey, you're the one who suggested I ride you."

The bear merely snorted in return and began to amble onward, then slowly quickened his pace. Aephrys held onto Charles's fur tightly so as not to fall. He grimaced at the stickiness the bear's coat put on his hands and made a mental note to give Charles a bath as soon as possible.

Once they got close to the tree Aephrys had been stuck in earlier, the dwarf heard bits of chattering and laughter coming from behind the tree line to his right.

"You hear that, Charles? It sounds like there are a bunch of people over there. Let's take a look."

Charles sauntered over into the direction of the voices, being as loud as he usually was, but once Aephrys saw what was before them, he hushed the bear.

"Stay hidden," he whispered, sliding off of his pet. He had to be especially careful not to land heavily while doing so, especially since he had quite a height to jump off of.

Aephrys tiptoed closer and kept himself hidden within the wide tree trunks, but he craned his neck around just enough to see what was before him: it was Nick and that girl... Oh, he couldn't remember her name. They were surrounded by about a dozen men astride some huge, menacing-looking horses— Aephrys never liked horses. They were too big and not nearly as smart as bears were.

An old, gray-haired man with a pathetic patch of scruff on his hollow cheeks that didn't even compare to Aephrys's beautiful beard, stood in the center. He commanded some of the men to take the huntsman and the girl. But that wasn't all that shocked Ae-phrys.

"Did he just call her the *Queen*?" the dwarf breathed. He threw his head in the direction of Charles hiding behind a bush that was much too small to cover up his large body. "She's the Queen!" he mouthed to the bear. But all he received in return was a cocked head and furry ears lifting in confusion.

Aephrys sighed and returned his attention back to the men kidnapping the huntsman and *the Queen*. As he watched the two of them get shoved behind another two men and their horses, the dwarf felt himself grow antsy. He started tapping his knobby fingers against the ground he crouched on, feeling like he had to do something. He held his breath as the party began to ride away and thought through all of his possible options.

"Charles!" he hissed over his shoulder. "We have to follow them!"

# Chapter 10

Dalia felt numb. She couldn't believe that she and Nick had been kidnapped, and it was all her fault. If she hadn't run off in the first place, none of this would be happening.

She darted her eyes about, trying to better look at the room they had been thrown in. It was musty, and the cold, stone floor was covered in bits of straw, but it was too dark to see more. About halfway through the two-hour trip, scratchy, woolen bags had been thrown over Nick and Dalia's heads to ensure they wouldn't know where they were headed. All she could determine was they were in a building of some sort, and they had been forced down a set of stairs to reach the room they were now sitting in.

Dalia flexed her hands against the thick cords tied around hers and Nick's wrists. Their hands were bound together in such a fashion that their backs were pressed against each other. The ropes were so tight that as she moved her wrists, they cut into her skin. She hissed at the pain and threw her head back against Nick's shoulder, trying not to cry from frustration.

"I'm sorry," she whispered to him. "I'm so sorry."

She felt the sides of his face hit her cheek as he

shook his head. "We'll get out of this, Dalia."

She snorted. "How? We're *tied up*, and they out-number us! Not to mention, they took away all of your weapons." Dalia allowed the tears to flow. "Who knows what they're planning on doing to us?" She tried to stop herself from imagining all of the terrible things the men could be capable of.

"They're probably putting you up for ransom," Nick reckoned. "I doubt they'll hurt you."

Dalia decided that Nick made a good point. Still, she had never been in a situation like this before, thankfully, but her lack of experience made her all the more frightened.

A stream of yellow light came past the staircase and into Dalia's eyes, making her have to squint at the sudden brightness. Heavy footsteps sounded as someone descended, making the wooden steps creak and groan precariously. As the newcomer approached, Dalia could see a stub of a candlestick glowing as a little flame danced on its frayed wick. She first took in the man; Dalia was better positioned than Nick to see as she faced the stairs, and he was facing behind her. The man entering was the leader from before with that same, menacing grin plastered onto his rugged face.

Dalia grimaced, trying to avoid the man's gray eyes and taking advantage of the newfound light to better study their surroundings. It was just as she suspected: an empty, stone-walled room that was barely large enough to fit the three of them.

"Ah, you're both awake."

Dalia narrowed her eyes at the man. How could they possibly sleep in such conditions?

"I'm Margrave Hurrey, by the way," he continued. "And of course I know who you are, my Queen," he leered in Dalia's direction. "But who are you?" he asked Nick.

Dalia could feel Nick's shoulder muscles stiffen.

"Why do you care?" Nick spat.

Margrave chuckled, which shook his gut in an unattractive fashion. "I don't. Just trying to make conversation. But I am fine sticking with 'huntsman' if you are."

Nick didn't answer, and the man merely shrugged. "Suit yourself, *huntsman*."

"Where are we?" Dalia demanded.

The old man wiggled his eyebrows. "You'd like to know that, wouldn't you? Well, that's for me to know and for you two *not* to know."

"Why are we here?" Nick began thrashing against their bindings, making Dalia yelp in discomfort as the cords cut through her flesh once again. "Are you trying to get rich off of kidnapping the *monarch* of Edristan?" Nick spat as far as he could, and his saliva actually reached the man's boots.

Margrave threw back his head and cackled. "You know, we will be getting rich, but it goes a lot further than just making demands for the Queen's return. We're going to start a war."

# Chapter 11

"Bring him in!" Margrave called over his shoulder.

Dalia was too shocked by the man's revelation of war to notice who Margrave was calling in. But all of the shuffling and shouts coming from the new prisoner snapped Dalia out of her reverie.

She gasped. "Frederik?"

The Prince of Wilaldan stood before them with hands clasped in front of him, and ropes tied around his own wrists. He had a black eye in the beginning stages of swelling with swirling hues of purples and was scraped up and bruised all over of his body. He was still in his bright white wedding garb from two days before, which suggested he had been taken before Dalia.

"Dalia?" he whispered. "Is that you?"

Nick perked up, shifting his body to the side to try and get a view of the newcomer. Dalia was in a better position to see than he was.

"*Prince* Frederik?" he blurted out. "You can't be serious!" Nick sounded almost… angry to learn of the Prince's arrival. Either he was shaken up by the Prince falling prey to these men, as well, or there was an underlying animosity he harbored for the Prince.

Dalia thought back to Nick saying something about the beautiful maiden he fell for, Snow White of all people, wanting to take the Prince away from the Queen. With that fact in mind, Dalia thought she could detect jealousy in Nick's voice. That made her stomach churn. Any recollections of Snow White, and the pain she had caused, always made Dalia feel ill, but for some reason, she found herself growing slightly envious of Snow White's hold on Nick. That surprised her because she usually felt that way when it came to Prince Frederik's past with the girl.

"What's going on?" Dalia demanded.

The little, stout man that had brought in the Prince shoved the prisoner onto the floor beside the other two. Margrave chuckled as Frederik hit the stone shoulder first and groaned in pain.

"We had a plan to kidnap you and the Prince right as you were leaving for your marriage tour. It was the perfect time with just the two of you riding in a carriage and flanked with merely a small entourage of guards. However..." Margrave licked his lips. "You made it very easy for us, Your Majesty. With that stunt you pulled at the wedding by running away. Your little Prince Frederik here—" He kicked a foot in the direction of the Prince. "He ran after you to bring you back, but we intercepted him along the way."

Dalia looked in her fiancé's direction, but he looked to the ground, avoiding her gaze. The Prince having gone after her when she left the wedding was surprising to Dalia, but she felt almost grateful and pleased to hear that he had been so noble.

"And all we had to do," he continued, "was find the lonely little Queen running off in the woods." Margrave flashed a sudden, angry look in Nick's direction. "We didn't plan on the huntsman coming along, so it took us a little longer to find you than we would have wanted, but..." The man's vile grin returned. "Here you are."

Dalia narrowed her eyes. "That doesn't explain how all of this kidnapping will start a war!"

Margrave and the other man shared glances and began laughing with one another.

"With you and the Prince missing, we have a few contacts within Edristan that will begin spreading rumors that Prince Frederik of Wilaldan wanted to turn against the marriage and took matters into his own hands by killing Queen Dalia Char of Edristan—his own betrothed."

Dalia gasped, and Frederik spat out blood onto the floor.

"No one will ever believe that!" Frederik cried.

"Oh," Margrave wiggled a finger in front of his pointed nose, "but they will." He slowly locked eyes with the Queen once again. "Especially once the people see their Queen's dead body and a still missing Prince Frederik. And then Edristan will definitely want to retaliate against the Kingdom of Wilaldan."

Dalia felt all the blood leave her face and didn't even notice the ropes rubbing against her skin as Nick struggled against them.

"You will not kill her!" The huntsman barked out

each word slowly, yet deliberately. "I won't let you!"

"*We* won't let you," Frederik added.

Margrave smirked and looked both young men up and down. "Yeah, you are both in a great position to stop us."

"Who wants this?" Dalia interjected. "Who wants to tear our kingdoms apart? Who do you work for?" When she should have continued to feel frightened, Dalia was surprised to find herself more concerned for her people and the other kingdoms. A war would be absolutely devastating.

Margrave snorted. He turned on his heel without replying and began climbing the staircase, the other man hobbling behind him.

"You answer me!" Dalia demanded. The light of Margrave's candlestick continued to fade as he retreated further and further away. "Who wants war?" she cried.

"Dalia," Nick whispered gently. "He's gone. You need to save your strength."

"For what?" the Queen scoffed.

"Because we are going to get out of here."

Dalia's lip began to tremble as she tried to turn her head to look at him. "How?"

"We'll find a way." It was Frederik's voice this time, but she couldn't see him anymore with the absence of the lit candle.

"We will." Nick was speaking again. "I promise."

Silence ensued between the three of them. Dalia's thoughts remained on the fear she felt. She didn't feel comforted by Nick and Frederik's promise to escape.

"I didn't think I'd ever see you again," Nick muttered under his breath, breaking the silence.

Dalia furrowed her brow and attempted to turn her head back to look at him. But before she could question what he had just said, Frederik chimed in:

"Nor I you."

Dalia let out a quick bark of laughter. "You two know each other?"

She couldn't see it in the darkness, but she could almost imagine Frederik's nod.

"I was enlisted to inform Nicholas of... a friend's death," the Prince said.

The way Frederik paused in the middle of the sentence made Dalia feel like he was hiding an important detail, but she didn't know if she cared much at that moment.

# Chapter 12

Margrave stood in front of his group of men with his hairy arms folded against his broad chest. Six of them were in the right corner of the main living area of the abandoned cabin their group had claimed. They were playing a game of dice and shouting out various bets of food and even clothing— none of them had money to bet with... *yet*. After this job was done, Margrave and his men would be rich beyond belief.

He moved his gaze to the other corner of the room where the rest of his men, excluding the two stationed outside to keep a lookout, were resting. The eight men were sprawled about on various parts of the floor, trying to get any bit of sleep they could. In fact, the thought of sleep was very appealing to Margrave. He couldn't remember the last time he had slept for more than a couple hours at a time. After getting hired for this job, he hadn't had time for rest between the planning and the kidnapping.

A thought Margrave had been pushing away was trying to present itself for the hundredth time that day: He still didn't know who had hired them; He didn't even know who *wanted* conflict between Edristan and Wilaldan. And of course, if war ensued between the two kingdoms, the other three were bound to join in.

When hired, the only contact Margrave had was a nameless, little man dressed in black, promising thousands of gold pieces for Margrave and his thieves' band to play out what his boss wanted. That boss was unknown to Margrave, but the more he thought about, and the more he imagined those beautiful gold pieces within his fingers, the more he really didn't care— not about who wanted a war, and not even about war itself.

Margrave extended his arms over his head and stretched, groaning slightly as some of his joints popped. He really was getting old. This job would be his last— he kept promising himself that. It helped that this final task would make him wealthy and set him up for the rest of his life.

"Sir?"

Margrave squinted his eyes shut and let out a long breath through his nose. He wasn't in the mood to be answering any of his men's questions at the moment.

"Yes, Gervaine?"

Gervaine, the youngest man in the group, rose from his resting position on the floor and hesitantly approached Margrave. Gervaine had been recruited to the thieves' band by Margrave just a year prior. He was eighteen then, and only nineteen now. Margrave couldn't remember why he decided the boy would be a good fit for their cunning robberies and plunderings— especially when he looked as pale and scared as he did in that moment.

Gervaine was wringing his hands together, brown eyes glued to the dusty, wooden floor.

"Sir?" His high voice grew even squeakier than usual as he lowered his volume. "Are we really planning on..." He dared to make eye contact with Margrave, but immediately shifted his gaze back to his feet. "Are we really going to kill them?"

Margrave felt his heart sink. Gervaine single-handedly was able to bring up the one thing that Margrave had been trying to convince himself he was fine with: the inevitable murders. Yes, he didn't care who hired him, and yes, he didn't even care about starting a war, but he had never taken someone's life with his own hands. They were a *thieves'* band, not killers. He and his men had done some terrible things, like leaving poor families destitute for the rest of their lives, or even beating men when trying to fight back. Still, they never went so far as to fatally harm a person.

"That's the plan," he finally said to the boy, trying to keep his face expressionless.

*Think of the money*, Margrave repeated in his mind over and over again.

Gervaine began shuffling his booted feet against the floor. He finally opened his mouth to say something, but he was interrupted by a loud roar coming from outside.

Margrave and every man in the room perked up to the sound.

"What the...?" Margrave muttered.

Aephrys stood a reasonable distance away, hidden behind a wide tree with his hands cupped tightly over his ears as Charles let out the loudest roar Aephrys had ever heard come from the bear. It was so loud, it hurt the dwarf's ears even with them covered, and the sound rumbled through the earth. Aephrys could have sworn he saw the leaves of the trees shake from the vibrations. The dwarf peeked out and watched as Charles threw his head back and continued to cry out. He even threw in a couple menacing growls here and there. The bear stood on his hindquarters and waved his claws up and down in a terrifying fashion.

Once the roaring stopped, the dwarf slowly took his hands off his ears and moved his head around the tree trunk to get a good look at what was happening. Two tall men— at least, Aephrys *thought* they were tall, not having the best frame of reference considering who and what he was— stood frozen at the doorway to a small cabin that looked rather worse for wear. Their square jaws were dropped nearly to the floor as they stared at the towering, black bear in front of them.

Aephrys saw Charles's head tilt to the side as he studied the men, noticing they weren't making a move to do anything.

"Alright," Aephrys breathed, "my turn."

Aephrys ignored the rough material of his tunic scratching against his skin as he straightened it. He then puffed out his chest and stood on the balls of his feet to look slightly taller as he came out from hiding and approached the scruffy men cowering before Charles. Neither of them didn't make a single move towards the rapiers and daggers tied at their sides.

Once he made it to the bear's side, Aephrys cleared his throat and shot a sideways glance at Charles. He could have sworn he saw the bear roll his big, brown eyes before returning to all fours. The animal was still massive and quite a bit bigger than the dwarf, but Charles going from two legs to all fours made Aephrys feel a little more confident.

"Gentlemen! This is my very good friend, Charles."

Aephrys gestured to the bear, and Charles grunted in response. The two men, one with nearly carrot-orange hair and patchy stubble, and the other extremely wide and red in the face, seemed to relax a little bit. Though, their eyes remained glued on the bear in front of them.

"W— who are you?" the chubby one stammered.

"I am Aephrys Greyforge," the dwarf bellowed, "and we are here to free your prisoners."

# Chapter 13

Dalia heard loud shuffling accompanied with stomps and cries from above. She craned her head up, noticing the wood of the floor above them beginning to creak and groan precariously. She could feel Nick squirming against the ropes tying their hands together.

"What's going on?" he whispered.

Dalia could hear Frederik shifting his position a couple of feet from her as his body scraped against the stone floor.

"It sounds like... It sounds like they're frightened," the Prince said.

Dalia felt her heart pounding in her chest. If there was someone, or something, those ruffians were fearful of, did that mean she and her fellow prisoners should be frightened, as well? She was already sick to her stomach knowing the men planned on murdering her but was there something worse up those stairs attacking her captors?

The three prisoners held their breaths as the scuffle continued above their heads, awaiting what seemed to be a terrible fate for themselves. Then all of a sudden, the sounds stopped. Dalia continued to hold her breath, even though she was beginning to feel lightheaded from lack of oxygen. Soon, the sound of the door at the top of the staircase swung open with a loud bang as it hit against the wall. Light from the upstairs poured in and blinded Dalia for a short period. She blinked repeatedly, trying to adjust to the light, then began peering up the stairs to see who was coming.

Heavy footfalls paraded down the steps, and Dalia could discern a large, dark form bumbling its way toward them. She yelped and tried to scurry away from it, but was restricted by Nick tied up against her back. But then she saw clearly:

"Charles!" she cried, tears of relief streaming down her face.

"A bear?" Frederik shouted. By the new light coming into the room, Dalia could see the Prince attempting to scramble up to his feet, but he seemed too sore from his scrapes and bruises to succeed.

"Ah, no need to worry." It was Aephrys's grumbly, old voice. "He's a friend."

Charles landed in front of the three to sit, causing a pile of dust to rise up in a cloud as his heavy rear landed with a thud. Dalia thought she could see a bit of a smile curling up under his thick coat of fur as the bear watched the three prisoners before him.

"What did you do?" Nick demanded, but the tone of his voice sounded relieved.

Aephrys shrugged, which was hard for Dalia to notice from the small amount of light, but she did all the same.

"Charles can be quite persuasive," he said.

Dalia shook her head. "But how? How did you know we were here?"

"We were on our way back to ask the huntsman where my seven nephews lived." Aephrys nodded in Nick's direction, making his long beard bounce. "And then we saw you two get taken by those thugs up there." The dwarf raised an eyebrow and turned in Frederik's direction. "And who is this?"

"How about we leave any more explanations for *after* we are untied and headed out of here?" Nick interjected.

"Oh, yes, yes. Of course."

Aephrys moved towards Nick and Dalia first and pulled out a dagger that he had hidden in his waistband. With a grin, he wiggled the thin blade in front of their faces.

"I took this off of one of those men up there. It's amazing the things you can do with a bear at your side— even as a dwarf."

"A dwarf?" Frederik cried. "Dwarves don't exist!"

Aephrys rolled his eyes, which seemed hard to do under his heavy, wrinkled eyelids. "Of course they do." He moved his attention back to Nick and Dalia. "Seriously, who is this guy?" He shifted his gaze back to the Prince and studied him with a deep scowl on his face. "And why is he dressed so... fancy?"

Dalia glanced over at Frederik and once again took in his wedding garb. Its stark whiteness had faded from dirt, and some of the ruffles were beginning to tear in places. Dalia opened her mouth to answer the dwarf as he began to cut hers and Nick's hands free, but Frederik got to it first:

"I am Prince Frederik of Wilaldan."

Aephrys paused in the middle of his sawing at the cords and slowly turned to Frederik.

"*Prince*?" His jaw dropped open, and he paused for a moment too long.

"I want to get out of here!" Nick snapped impatiently.

Aephrys shook his head with a chuckle as he continued to cut Nick and Dalia free.

"In the presence of the Queen and a Prince. Quite a day, if I do say so myself."

Dalia sighed in relief as she felt her hands go free and began rubbing her sore wrists. She was too happy about not being tied up anymore that she almost didn't notice what the dwarf had said.

"Wait," Dalia hesitated, "How do you know I am the Queen?"

Aephrys shrugged as he shuffled over to free Frederik. "I heard the men say it when they were taking you into custody."

Nick leapt up from the floor and hollered out joyfully as he stretched. "Let's go!"

Dalia and Frederik, *especially* Frederik, were not as quick to get up. Dalia felt sore from sitting on the cold, stone floor for so many hours, and she could hear Frederik quietly groaning in pain from his injuries as he tried to rise. For the first time, the Queen was beginning to feel sympathetic towards the Prince. She began to remember the period, though short it had been, when she found him handsome and even took quite a liking to him. Had she been too rash in running off from their wedding?

Then, for some reason, Dalia's mind wandered to the handsome, mysterious huntsman she had met almost two days before: How he had protected her, helped her, and how he was even starting to warm up to her. The Queen turned to look in Nick's direction and found herself studying the sharpness of his jaw and the angles in his cheeks and how his brown bangs fell in front of his brooding eyes.

Before Dalia could notice that she had been staring for a little too long, Nick glanced over at her. She felt her face grow warm and tried to cover her cheeks with her hands, then realized in relief that it was probably too dark for him to have noticed her staring or even her face turning red.

"Why aren't we leaving?" Nick demanded, sprinting towards the stairs. Suddenly, he halted and slowly turned around at the bottom of the steps. "Uh, are they..."

"Dead?" Aephrys chuckled, the sound rumbling deep in his chest. "Of course not. Just scared out of their wits."

# Chapter 14

Dalia reached the top of the steps after all of the men and the bear. Nick, Aephrys, and Charles bounded through the doorway without a worry, but it took Frederik a bit longer to pass the threshold as he was grabbing at his side and breathing heavily through the pain he was feeling. Once they had all entered the upstairs room, the Queen cautiously peeked her head around the doorframe. She saw a small living area, with a fireplace that was only about a foot wide, and empty walls with the paint having chipped off long ago. Upon further study, Dalia concluded they were in a cabin that had long been abandoned.

She moved her eyes to all of the vandals that had taken her captive. Every last one of them was lined up and had their backs to the wall, including Margrave. Dalia was still tentative to enter the room with all of them in there watching, but once she saw the look of fear plastered on their faces as they watched the massive, black bear pace the floor in front of them with a growl in his throat, she felt herself relax and dared to step through.

"You just got lucky, Your Majesty!" Margrave spat.

Dalia glanced over at the leader and began trembling slightly at the look of fury raging in his dark eyes.

"There are people who will not stop until this war starts, and you won't always have a blasted *bear* to help you."

The Queen felt her own rage flare up inside of her as the man spoke. She urged her knees to stop wobbling and approached Margrave, shoving her nose right up against his own. Her courage surprised even herself as she glared at the old man with her jaw set and narrow shoulders straight as an arrow.

"How dare you," she growled. "How *dare* you speak to me in such a way."

She could feel the eyes of her companions watching her, shocked, from behind.

"If I were you, I would leave right now. Out of Edristan— maybe even outside of the five kingdoms. Go to Lurid, for all I care! But if you and your men *ever* come back..." Dalia gave a lengthy pause and sneered at Margrave. She edged herself even closer to him and could smell his foul breath. Margrave pressed himself tighter against the wall, and the Queen was pleased to see his body shake slightly from fear. "I will not be so merciful."

Before she allowed the man to contribute even one word of an answer, she spun on her heel and faced her companions. Each of them had their mouths hanging open as they stared at her. She noticed, in particular, the look of awe shining in Nick's sea-green eyes. She darted her own eyes away, trying to stop herself from flushing a deep red.

"Let's get out of here," she said.

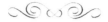

Margrave watched as his prisoners left with that little dwarf and his bear. He was too shocked to move as they retreated from the cabin. Shocked by the appearance of a dwarf and his pet bear, for one thing. Margrave knew of the existence of dwarves, of course, having been in the mountains of Lurid many times in his life, but one having the companionship of a giant, black bear was more than odd. Actually, it was strange for *any* type of person.

But the large animal wasn't the most surprising occurrence; He had been told Queen Dalia did not have a single courageous bone in her body. He had obviously been given false information. As the small group left through the front doorway that had been forcefully widened by the bear upon its initial entrance, Margrave slammed his fist against the wall. The impact made the entire building shake slightly atop its precarious foundation.

"What should we do, sir?"

Margrave was barely able to hear Gervaine's voice over his own tumultuous thoughts. But once he processed the boy's words, he stepped in front of his line of men with fists shoved on his hips and feet planted firmly shoulder-width apart.

"We are not going to let them get away!" Margrave

shouted. "If we put our minds to it, there is no way even a bear can defeat us— *especially* with our numbers." He spat on the floor to his right. "We're cowards to have let it sway us before! Who is with me?"

Each man seemed to inhale a single, sharp breath simultaneously and shift their eyes to their feet. Some nervous chattering began, and Margrave's hands faltered from his hips and fell to his sides. Served him right for putting his trust and livelihood in the hands of a bunch of thieves.

"Are you really all that daft and spineless? What about the money?"

"I'll go with you, sir."

A hush fell upon the room as Gervaine stepped forward. He puffed out his chest and clenched his fists, trying desperately to look braver and older.

"You've always wanted me to prove myself to you, Margrave," Gervaine continued. "I think going after the Queen is a good way to do that."

Margrave looked the scrawny boy up and down. The filthy clothing on Gervaine's body was noticeably large on him, and his boyish, round face didn't give Margrave any sense of hope that the young man could provide much assistance.

"Alright," Margrave said reluctantly. "Anyone else?"

After many seconds of silence, two other men raised their hands and approached Margrave and Gervaine's sides. It was Andrew and Randolph, the two that Margrave had first recruited in the very beginning— they had always been loyal to him, and it seemed they didn't plan on stopping now.

Margrave attempted to make eye contact with his other men, but they all avoided his gaze. The anger Margrave felt at not only his men, but at the situation of letting the Queen go and possibly losing all of that gold was about to make him boil over. He clenched and unclenched his fists as one thief after another turned red and refused to look up at him.

"Suit yourselves! Go home, and don't expect any share of the gold from me!"

Without another word, Margrave stormed out of the cabin, clutching the rapier at his side and gesturing with his free hand for the few men brave enough to follow.

# Chapter 15

It was beginning to grow dark outside as the five of them, including the bear, traveled further and further away from the group of thugs. Dalia grinned up at the sky as thousands of stars slowly began to appear and twinkle among the few wisps of clouds.

As the group walked, Prince Frederik was beginning to fall behind. His breathing became rapid, and his limp grew stronger than before.

"I'm sorry!" he called. "Don't worry about me— I'll catch up!"

The entire group stopped and looked back at the Prince. Dalia pursed her lips in worry. The poor man. How long had they been beating him? And why? Had they been punishing him for fighting back? Were they trying to break him?

Charles grunted and cantered over to Frederik, bending close to the forest floor and nudging the Prince with his head.

"Uh," Frederik eyed the dwarf, "what's it doing?"

"*He*," Aephrys emphasized. "Charles is a 'he.' And I think he's offering for you to ride him."

Dalia was still amazed by the bear's intelligence and ability to interact with humans as he allowed Prince Frederik to scramble onto his back. The group then continued on their way, Aephrys walking beside his pet and rambling on about how to correctly hammer at stone and precious metals in the mountains. Frederik seemed to be trying to listen, but he silently groaned from pain and seemed to be slowly drifting off to sleep. Nick and Dalia trailed behind, standing about a shoulder's width away from one another.

"You were incredible back there," Nick said, breaking the awkward silence.

The Queen's lips twitched into a smile. "I didn't know I had it in me."

"I did." Nick smiled back at her as they walked. "I noticed that fire in you from the moment we met."

Dalia's heart skipped a beat from the compliment. She once again noticed how ruggedly handsome Nick looked under the moonlight. She then noticed that he was staring, too. The Queen cleared her throat and brushed off his words with a chuckle.

"People don't really say those kinds of things to me," she whispered. "Especially not after my parents' and my friend Aeryn's deaths."

Dalia shifted her head to her feet and watched as her boots slid through the piles of dead leaves and grass on the trail.

"I'm so sorry."

Nick gingerly brushed the tips of his fingers against Dalia's shoulder. The Queen stopped as he touched her, and Nick halted, as well. They stared into each other's eyes, both sharing in a certain solemnity.

"Snow White killed her," Dalia blurted out.

Nick took his hand off of the Queen's shoulder as if he had just been stung. "What?"

"She was trying to kill me, but instead, she killed my friend."

Nick dropped his eyes to his feet, then slowly placed his face in his hands. Dalia thought she must have misheard at first, but as she moved closer to better listen, she could hear his soft sobs muffled by the huntsman's dirt-covered hands.

"Nick?" she inquired. Dalia was taken aback by his emotion, not having pictured him the type to cry.

"That's terrible," he choked. "I can't believe... I can't believe I tried so hard for so long to only see the good in her." Nick looked up from his hands and gave Dalia a small smile. Her heart ached for him as she saw a tear stuck to his cheek. "Thank you. Thank you for telling me. I think it will help me finally move on."

Dalia's body twitched as she tried to decide whether or not to embrace the huntsman, but then she shrugged her hesitation away and decided to do so. She threw her arms around his neck and squeezed him tight.

"No, thank *you*," she whispered in his ear. "Without you, I would not have survived the last couple of days."

Slowly, Nick's arms wrapped around Dalia's slender waist. He then buried his face in her tangled curls and let the tears come harder. Dalia cried with him as they continued to embrace, feeling comforted by the warmth of his body.

"Hey!"

Dalia and Nick separated from one another quickly as Aephrys hollered back at them. The dwarf had a bushy, white eyebrow raised nearly all the way up to his hairline at the two of them. Even the Prince was looking back at them with a question on his lips. Dalia flushed a deep red and hiked up her skirts, ready to sprint after the three who had gotten so far ahead. But just as she put one foot down to begin catching up, she felt rough hands clasp tightly around her mouth. She tried to scream, but her voice was muffled against the stranger's hand.

The Queen looked in Nick's direction and saw that he had been restrained by three other men. He struggled against them, trying to reach for any of his weapons that he had retrieved before leaving the abandoned cabin, but such efforts were fruitless against the three. Though one of them seemed about the same age as Dalia and was short and scrawny, the other two were very burly and strong.

Dalia vaguely recognized the bearded, square jaws and dark clothing. She concluded they were from the group that had taken them before. She tried to stretch her neck around to see her captor, but the man had his arms pressed so tightly against her, she couldn't budge even an inch.

"You get off of them!" she heard Aephrys cry, but they were so far ahead that the dwarf, bear, and the Prince couldn't reach them before the man behind her took one hand away from her mouth to unsheath a large knife, then pressed it against her throat.

"Don't you come any closer!" the man growled.

Dalia sank sorrowfully into her captor's grip, recognizing the voice immediately. It was Margrave.

"I will slice her throat right here if you make any move to save her!" he continued.

Dalia whimpered, her arms tight against her sides. She could taste the dirt on his sweaty palm as he squeezed both the hand on her mouth and the knife against her neck tighter. She could feel the blade break a small piece of skin and felt bits of warm liquid trickle down her front as it bled.

Charles began growling and snapping his jaw, but Aeprhys held a hand up to keep the bear from charging forward.

"What do you want?" Dalia choked. "Do you want money? I'm the *Queen*— I can give you money. Just name your price!"

Before Margrave could answer, the sound of an arrow whistled loudly in Dalia's ears and landed with a twang in the hand he held the knife in. Margrave cried out and dropped the Queen out of his grip, clutching his injured hand as he continued to holler out in pain. Dalia lost her balance as he released her and fell to the ground, but she caught herself with her hands and winced as the small rocks and bits of twigs cut into her palms.

The three men holding Nick down looked around, confused, which caused them to relax a bit on their grip. Nick took the opportunity to push out of their hands and pull out his hatchet on them. The three men moved to retrieve their own weapons, but before they could retain Nick again, Aephrys commanded Charles to run forward. Frederik was still on the bear's back, and he was nearly thrust off as the animal charged, but the Prince tightened his grip on Charles's fur to keep himself steady.

The bear let out a roar that rumbled so loudly, Dalia could feel vibrations coming from the forest floor and through her body. Margrave remained curled up in a ball just a couple of feet away from her, rolling and shouting in agony as blood streamed out of the wound in his hand and down the wood of the arrow. As the Queen looked at the arrow, she cocked her head to the side and studied it, beginning to recognize its white color and inlays of gold thread circling the shaft. It was a royal Edristan arrow.

Dalia leapt to her feet excitedly and thrashed her head about to find the source of the arrow. Suddenly, a line of half a dozen white horses flooded into the area and circled the party. She felt her shoulders slump forward in relief. It was a group of castle soldiers! Each man was clad in the kingdom's blue and white colors underneath a pile of silver armor that glinted as the moonlight hit each piece. One of the soldiers had his longbow in hand rather than strapped to his back like the other men. Dalia smiled; He must have been the source of the shot.

"Thank goodness you're all here!" she exclaimed.

The one with the bow in hand gave a charming smile and flipped his shoulder-length, blond hair out of his face.

"Everyone has been worried sick, Your Majesty," he said.

A sense of relief rushed through the Queen's body. It was so powerful that she almost couldn't handle it and fell once again to the forest floor. She was going home.

# Chapter 16

Dalia sat at the head of the long table in the castle's main study. Short bookcases lined the walls to her side and behind. A long door with the leafless tree emblem of Edristan carved delicately into its white-painted wood stood mightily in front of her. The Queen studied the elegant carving of the precise lines in the tree's bark as it twisted up into its many branches. She had never thought the leafless tree emblem to represent strength before, but as she sat at the head of a long, wooden table before a large group of men, she could almost feel the tree supporting her.

Surrounding her on each side were her ten royal advisors. They were all ancient, stuffy men with noses pointed up into the air, and wrinkled faces frowning deeply. To her right was her primary advisor, Lord Magnus. His bald head reflected the glow of the candlelight around them as he turned to her and gave her a smile, chapped lips splitting in various places from the movement.

Lord Magnus was the royal advisor for her parents before their untimely death. He had only recently appointed the other nine men under the argument that a young queen, such as Dalia, needed more wise minds surrounding her. But the reason they all had to be ancient, old men, she didn't quite understand.

Nick sat near the end of the table, having had put two seats between himself and the closest person. Dalia had asked for him to attend this meeting, much to the advisors' chagrin.

Nick still wore the clothing on the day Dalia had met him, with his brown cloak tied around his worn tunic and trousers. But two things were different: one of the servants must have cleaned them for him because they were much less stained with dirt. His weapons were also not on his person at the moment. He shifted uncomfortably in his seat, obviously feeling out of place.

Yes, Nick's attire was starkly different next to the ruffles and colorful tunics the advisors wore, but Dalia was envious of him. She looked down at her own dark green gown and silently began wishing away the hoop skirt and scratchy lace. She was glad to be home, clean, and away from any men trying to kill her, but sometimes she missed the comforts of not worrying about appearances and being out in the woods without a care in the world.

The royal advisors had given Dalia a week to settle back in and recover from any trauma she might have experienced in those few days away from the castle. She was grateful for the time they gave her, but they insisted she call a meeting on how to go forward after the week of rest— especially after she had explained the reason for her kidnapping. She had agreed to a meeting but also insisted they listen to her and allow Nick to stay in the castle for a while. It took quite a bit of urging, but they finally relented. Dalia had made a mental note that she needed to figure out how to get it through to her advisors that *she* was the monarch— not them.

Aephrys and his bear were long gone. After receiving generous compensation for their assistance and receiving directions from Nick, they went off to find the dwarf's seven nephews days ago. But Nick had stayed, and he and the Queen had been spending a lot of time together within the past week. She watched as Nick twiddled his thumbs nervously at the end of the table. He noticed and gave her a warm smile. Quiet contentment filled Dalia's heart as she returned the smile. She remembered fondly of his promise to walk the grounds with her again once this meeting had finished.

"Ahem." Lord Magnus's gravelly voice echoed in the spacious study. "I believe we should get started."

Dalia cleared her throat and quickly broke eye contact with Nick. "Of course."

Lord Magnus clasped his hands together and set them on the table in front of him. "How about you start from the beginning."

Dalia opened her mouth to begin, but then noticed the absence of a particular person.

"Where is Prince Frederik?"

Each advisor shared solemn, knowing glances with one another.

"Uh, he left, Your Majesty. This morning."

The Queen furrowed her brow and looked back at

Lord Magnus. "Why?"

"He said something about…" The Lord looked in Nick's direction. "About not wanting to be in your way anymore."

Dalia froze, not knowing what to say to that. She opened and closed her mouth to reply, but no words came out. She shook her head and decided to change the subject:

"Before I begin telling you what happened last week, I wish to announce something."

All of the men, including Nick, sat up on the edge of their seats.

Dalia nodded towards Nick. "I want to appoint Nicholas Smith as our royal huntsman."

Nick's jaw dropped open, and silence fell upon the room. It was broken by a few snickers from her advisors.

"A *royal* huntsman?" the one closest to Nick guffawed. "But we get all of our game from the market."

The Queen lifted her chin in response. "There will be no more discussion. Nicholas should be rewarded for his assistance towards me, and this new title is how I have chosen to do just that."

All of the men looked shocked. Dalia had never stood up for herself in such a way before, but she was determined that they would have to start getting used to it. She dared a look in Nick's direction and relaxed as she saw a pleased look on his face.

"And now I will start from the beginning of my tale. First, you all saw what happened at the wedding, of course."

And then she told them everything. Well, as much as she wanted to without embarrassing herself. She explained her running away as succumbing to wedding jitters and told them about Nick's kindness and the help he provided. She then moved on to the thieves' band.

"And as I said to you before, they were hired to start a war," she continued.

Many of the advisors nodded, but a few began chattering nervously.

"Do you know who hired them?" a little man with a powdered wig atop his pointy head asked.

She shook her head. "As far as I know, even *they* were not aware."

Lord Magnus tapped his fingers against the table as he thought. "We need to send our best spies out on this immediately. Worry not, my Queen. We will learn who wants this war and put a stop to any more of this disastrous mischief."

Dalia gave a curt nod in response.

"Now, in regards to a match for you," the Lord added.

The Queen raised an eyebrow. "You mean, a husband?"

He bobbed his head up and down in a 'yes.' "You need to have a King by your side to effectively rule Edristan. Especially with all this talk of a threat of war."

"No, I don't."

The advisors all gasped in unison at her response,

but she continued:

"I will marry when I want to— not for politics, not because I have to, but because I fell in love."

Dalia glanced quickly at Nick. His smile from before grew even bigger, and Dalia bit her lip to suppress a giggle.

"But—"

She held up a finger at Lord Magnus. "There will be no discussion on that topic, either." Dalia stood up gingerly and brushed down her skirts to straighten them out. "Shall we go take a stroll in the gardens now, Nick?"

The royal huntsman pushed his own chair back much less gracefully than Dalia had, but he didn't seem to care.

"We shall," he replied.

"Meeting adjourned," Dalia said to the advisors.

She then approached Nick with her head held high and wrapped her arm in the crook of one of his own. They stepped out of the study together, leaving the confused old men behind.

———————

# Note from the Author

Thank you for taking the time to read my book! I hope you enjoyed it. If you did, spreading the word would be much appreciated! For instance, leaving an Amazon or Goodreads review, or sharing on social media, would make all the difference! Subscribe to my newsletter and take a look at my website to receive updates, book releases, and so much more!

Newsletter: http://eepurl.com/g-ioqz
Site: https://aleesehughes.com

Be sure to follow me on all social medias:
Instagram: @aleesehughes
Facebook: Aleese Hughes
Twitter: @AleeseHughes

# Map

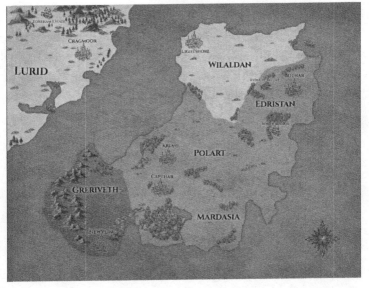

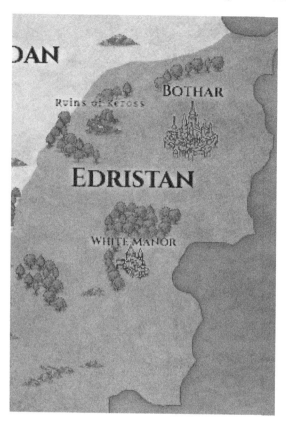

# About the Author

Aleese Hughes is many things: a mother and wife, an avid reader, a performer, and an author. Aleese enjoys her time at home with her children and relishes the opportunities to pick up a good book or write one herself.

Having grown up around theater her entire life, Aleese has a natural ability when it comes to charming audiences while on stage. And the same goes for her knack to put words to paper and create stories that people of all ages can read and enjoy.

The fantasy genre is not only her favorite to read, but it is also what she writes, including "The Tales and Princesses Series," and "After the Tales and Princesses- A Set of Novellas."

# More by Aleese Hughes

## *The Tales and Princesses Series*

Book 1: Peas and Princesses

Book 2: Apples and Princesses

Book 3: Pumpkins and Princesses

Book 4: Beasts and Princesses

## *After the Tales and Princesses*
## *— A Set of Novellas*

Novella 1: Janice Wallander: A Novella Retelling the Tale of Rumpelstiltskin

Novella 2: Queen Dalia Char: A Novella Retelling the Tale of Rose Red

Made in the USA
Monee, IL
13 November 2023

46425974R00062